Mar

Some South African nursery rhymes
for you, Isla, on your christening day.

With love & best wishes,

The Cahill family
X

To my parents, Bill and Meg Collier, and to my grandchildren:

Joshua, Melissa, Jack, Harry, Lia, Rosie, Jude, and those still to be born.

AFRICAN NURSERY RHYMES

Liz Mills

Introduction

Nursery rhymes sung or recited by adults to young children are part of a tradition as old as mankind, although their very age might obscure their meaning.

The jingles, counting rhymes, lullabies and riddles that constitute the rhymes introduce the child to concepts that are essential to its navigation through life. Food, body parts, numbers, colours and the relationship of the child to others and its surroundings: this is the stuff that makes up the rhymes. Through them the child appreciates humour and learns a sense of rhythm and a love for music. Above all, their psychological benefit to both child and adult is considerable. Parents know that a nursery rhyme can give comfort to a distressed child, that a lullaby can lull a grizzly baby to sleep. They forge a close and exclusive bond between the child and its carer and provide an ideal opportunity for a cuddle!

Nursery rhymes that are part of a literary tradition often give a child its first introduction to the printed and illustrated page and instill in it a love of books and the library.

The rhymes that appear in the following pages are grounded in the English nursery rhyme tradition. However, they have been given a South African flavour, offering our children a taste of our warm rich land, filled as they are with recognizable South African images with which the child can identify.

South Africa is a land of many cultures, all of which have a rich tradition of nursery rhymes. These rhymes are part of our collective national heritage. We owe it to successive generations of South Africans to collect and preserve them, thereby ensuring that they move from the periphery to the centre of our children's imagination.

Tanya Barben
Rare Books Librarian and Curator, South African Children's Literature Collection, University of Cape Town Libraries.

Hey diddle dimba, giraffe and marimba,
The springbok jumped over the moon.
The hyena laughed to see such fun,
And the pot ran away with the spoon!

Neo and Kay went to the vlei
To fetch a bucket of water.
Kay saw a rock, upon which sat a croc,
Which chased her and nearly caught her!

Naledi, Naledi, it's spring already.
How does your garden grow?
With silver rain and golden grain,
And mealie stalks all in a row.

Rock-a-bye baby tied in a rug,
When Mama walks the baby is snug,
When Mama trips, the baby goes bump,
And down will go baby and Ma with a thump!

Two little oxpeckers sat upon a gnu,
One named Thabo and one named Sue.
Fly away Thabo, fly away Sue!
Come back Thabo, come back Sue!

Pussycat, pussycat, where did you go?
I went to Madiba to say: 'Hello!'
Pussycat, pussycat, what did you see?
I saw him sitting and having his tea!

Lehe-lehe sat on a wall,
Lehe-lehe had a great fall,
And all of the ostriches, one to ten,
Could not put Lehe together again!

Come little herder, whistle and shout!
There are sheep in the veggies,
the cows have got out!
Where is the little boy who looks after the sheep?
He's under the thorn tree, fast asleep.

Sing a song of five cents,
A pocket full of rye,
Four and twenty hadedas,
Baked in a pie.
When the pie was opened,
The birds began to call;
Oh, how they screamed and squawked,
It did annoy us all.

Dad was at the ATM,
Drawing out some money.
Mom was in the kitchen,
Eating toast and honey.
Gran was in the garden,
Hanging out the clothes,
When along came a hadeda
And pecked off her nose!

Tom, Tom the headman's son,
Stole a pig and away he run.
The pig was caught and Tom was taught,
Stealing is wrong – of any sort!

There was an old woman who lived in a shoe,
She had so many children
She didn't know what to do.
So she wiped all their faces
And dressed them in jeans
And gave them big bowls
Of cold samp and beans.

Doctor Letholi went to Egoli
In a shower of rain.
He stepped in a puddle, right up to his middle
And never went there again!

Little Miss Mary found it quite scary,
While eating her porridge one day.
A big, hairy spider jumped down beside her
And frightened Miss Mary away!

Tickety, tickety, tock,
The mouse ran up the clock.
The clock struck one, the mouse ran down,
Tickety, tickety, tock.

Bing, bong, bam, kitty's in the dam.

Who put her in? Little Johnny Slim.

Who took her out? Little Sipho Stout.

What a naughty boy was that,

To try and drown poor kitty cat,

Who never did him any harm,

But caught the rats in Oupa's barn.

Roll, roll, roll the dung
Safely down the road.
Steadily, steadily, steadily, steadily –
Such a heavy load!

Roll, roll, roll the dung
In a ball so neat.
Wrong way round, upside down –
Push it with your feet!

Roll, roll, roll the dung
Right up to your nest.
Set it down, turn around –
Go back and fetch the rest!

Little Lebo Long Legs runs down the street.
This side and that side on his bare feet.
Knocking at the window, tapping at the lock;
Are the children in their beds? It's now eight o'clock.

Katie put the kettle on,
Katie put the kettle on,
Katie put the kettle on,
We'll all have tea!

Neo take it off again,
Neo take it off again,
Neo take it off again,
They've all gone away!

Ten little Rainbow people walking in a line.
An elephant sat on one ...
Then there were nine!

Nine little Rainbow people thought they would be late.
The taxi left one behind ...
Then there were eight!

Eight little Rainbow people –
One of them was Kevin.
He stopped to tie his shoe ...
Then there were seven!

Seven little Rainbow people stopped to pick up sticks.
A baboon took one by the hand ...
Then there were six!

Six little Rainbow people
Tried to rob a hive.
A bee stung one on the nose ...
Then there were five!

Five little Rainbow people heard a lion roar.
Thandi stopped to look around ...
Then there were four!

Four little Rainbow people
Climbing up a tree.
A branch broke!
Oopsy-daisy ...
Then there were three!

Three little Rainbow people
tasted Mama's brew.
One had a sip too much ...
Then there were two!

Two little Rainbow people playing in the sun.
One forgot his sunscreen ...
Then there was one!

One little Rainbow person saw the day was done.
Went to bed so sleepy ...
Then there were none!

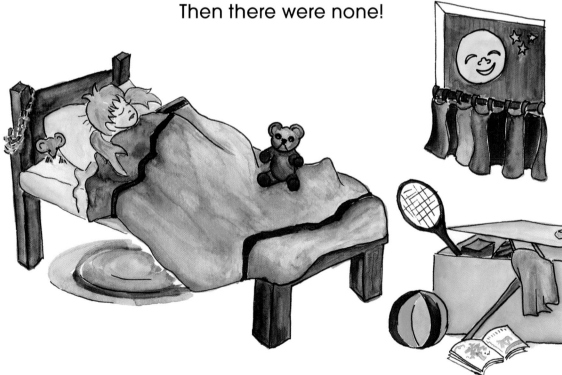

Bongi Bo Peep has lost her sheep,
Way out in the vast Karoo.
Leave them alone and they'll come home,
And their tails will follow them too!

Thuto, Thuto, biltong and braai,
Kissed the girls and made them cry.
When the boys came out to play,
Thuto, Thuto ran away!

The grand old Zulu king
He had ten thousand men;
He marched them up the Drakensberg,
And he marched them down again.
And when they were up, they were up,
And when they were down, they were down,
And when they were only halfway up,
They were neither up nor down.

Hurry up! Hurry up! Pizza man!
Make us a pizza as fast as you can!
Roll it and bake it and mark it in three,
Ready for Pule, Farieda and me.

This is the house that Thabo built.
These are the mealies that lay
in the house that Thabo built.
This is the rat that ate the mealies
That lay in the house that Thabo built.

This is the cat that caught the rat
That ate the mealies that lay
in the house that Thabo built.
This is the dog that chased the cat
That caught the rat that ate the mealies
That lay in the house that Thabo built.

Mary had a little lamb,
Its wool was white as snow,
And everywhere that Mary went,
The lamb was sure to go.

It followed her to school one day,
Which was against the rule.
It made the children laugh and clap
To see a lamb at school.

One, two, three, four, five,
Once I caught a fish alive.
Six, seven, eight, nine, ten,
Then I let it go again.
Why did you let it go?
Because it bit my finger so.
Which finger did it bite?
It bit my pinkie on the right.

It's raining, it's pouring, Ntate is snoring.
He went to bed with no teeth in his head,
And hoped they'd be there in the morning!

Chakalaka hot, chakalaka cold,
Chakalaka in the pot, nine days old!

I had a little baobab,
Nothing would it bear,
But an orange naartjie
And a silver pear.
The Xhosa king's daughter
Came to visit me,
And all for the sake
Of my baobab tree.

Poor Oom Piet could eat no meat,
His wife could eat no bean.
So between them both, you see,
They scraped the potjie clean.

This little warthog
went out shopping.

This little warthog
stayed at home.

This little warthog
ate ice cream.

This little warthog
had none.

And this little warthog went
'Eish, eish, eish!' all the way home.

Monday's child is fair of face.
Tuesday's child is full of grace.
Wednesday's child is full of woe.
Thursday's child has far to go.
Friday's child is loving and giving.
Saturday's child works hard for a living.

But a child that is born on the Sabbath day,
Is happy and good and loves to play.

How many roads to Cape Town?
Many hundreds and ten!
Can we get there by taxi?
Yes – and back again!

Jabulani went to town
Riding on an ellie.
He put a feather in his cap,
And called it jelly belly!

The man in the moon came down too soon,
And asked his way to Durban.
He rode in on a goat, wearing a coat,
And a very bright purple turban!

Rub-a-dub-ducket, three men in a bucket,
And who do you think they are?
A pilot, a farmer, a sangoma charmer;
They all fell out of a rotten banana,
And tried to fly to a star.

Ladybird, ladybird fly away home,
Your house is on fire, your children all gone.
All except one and that's little Bill.
He has crept under the braaivleis grill.

Little Sipho Small
Is not very tall ...
If he did not have his hat on
We would not see him at all!

Girls and boys come out to play,
The moon it shines as bright as day.
Leave your supper and leave your sleep,
And join your playmates in the street.
Come with a bat and come with a ball,
And come to play cricket or not at all!

One cheerful summer morning,
When sunny was the weather,
There I met an old man,
All dressed up in feathers.
He began to wave and nod
And I began to grin.
How do you do? And how do you do?
And how do you do again?

Ride a fat pony way out to Benoni,
To see a huge hippo eat hot macaroni.
With rings through his ears and bells on his toes,
He shall have music wherever he goes!

Squeaky, squawky guinea fowl hen,
Do you lay eggs for all good men?
Hungry men will come and pay
For eggs laid fresh on every day.
Sometimes nine and sometimes ten,
Squeaky, squawky guinea fowl hen.

Big **A**, little a, great bouncing **B**,
The lion's in the cupboard and can't see me!

Do you know the mealie lady,
mealie lady, mealie lady?
Do you know the mealie lady,
who walks down Jozi's streets?

Old Mama Hubbard went to the cupboard
To get her poor dog a treat.

When she opened the tin –
meerkats had got in ...
And so he had nothing to eat.

She went to the spaza
to get him some beans ...
But when she got back
he was wearing her jeans!

She went to the butcher
to get him some wors ...
But when she got back
he was riding a horse!

She could not find a thing
that he liked at all ...
So he put on his hat
and went off to the mall!

The lion and the crocodile were fighting for the prey,
Across the plains of Africa one dry and sunny day.
The lion said: 'It's my buck!'
The croc he said: 'No way!'
And while they both were fighting,
the buck ran off to play!

What are little boys made of, made of?
What are little boys made of?
Mopanis, snails and lion cub tails,
That's what little boys are made of.

What are little girls made of, made of?
What are little girls made of?
Butterflies, bows and pink pointy toes,
That's what little girls are made of.

There was a crooked man,
And he walked a crooked way,
He found a crooked five cents
One sunny, crooked day.
He had a crooked cat
That caught a crooked mouse.
And they all lived together
In a crooked little house!

Baa baa black sheep, have you any wool?
Yes sir, yes sir, three bags full!
One for the farmer and one bag to sell,
And one for the workers on the farm as well!

Little Rasool sat on a stool
Eating a chicken pie.
He chomped and he chewed and ate all his food,
And said: 'What a good boy am I!'

Diddle, diddle, doughnut, my son John,
Went to bed with a headdress on.
One feather right, and the other feather wrong;
Diddle, diddle, doughnut, my son John!

Twinkle, twinkle little star,
How I wonder what you are?
Up above the world so high,
Southern Cross shine in the sky.
Twinkle, twinkle little star,
How I wonder what you are?

Go to sleep my baby, close your pretty eyes.
Angels up above you, watching from the skies,
Great big moon is shining, stars begin to peep,
Time for little boys and girls to go to sleep.

Author's acknowledgements
Thanks to my family for encouraging me to submit the rhymes.
Thanks also to Linda de Villiers, Joy Clack and Janine Damon for their help.
And to Larry, for his support and interest.

Struik Lifestyle
(an imprint of Random House Struik (Pty) Ltd)
Company Reg. No. 1966/003153/07
80 McKenzie Street, Cape Town 8001
PO Box 1144, Cape Town, 8000, South Africa

First published in 2006 by Struik Publishers
Reprinted in 2007, 2008
Reprinted by Struik Lifestyle in 2009

Publisher: Linda de Villiers
Editor: Joy Clack
Designer: Janine Damon
Illustrator: Liz Mills
Proofreader: Irma van Wyk

Reproduction: Hirt & Carter Cape (Pty) Ltd
Printing and binding: Times Offset (M) Sdn Bhd

ISBN 978-1-77007-253-4

www.imagesofafrica.co.za

IMAGES OF AFRICA
PHOTO LIBRARY

Over 40 000 unique African images available
to purchase from our image bank at
www.imagesofafrica.co.za